the WOODS

Rob Hodgson

Frances Lincoln
Children's Books

Here are the woods. The woods are home to three foxes.

Three foxes that are on a hunt...

...for rabbits.

Tasty, delicious rabbits.

Luckily, someone has shown them the way to go.

They search over the tallest trees.

'No rabbits up here,' says Tiny Fox.

And under the carrot fields.

'No rabbits down there,' says Tiny Fox.

And through the
pumpkin patch.

'There are only pumpkins
in this pumpkin patch,'
says Tiny Fox.

That evening the three foxes wonder if
they'll ever catch a rabbit.

'Maybe hunting doughnuts would be easier,'
says Round Fox.

'And I could hunt acorns,' says Tall Fox.

'NO!' says Tiny Fox. 'We are foxes.
We must capture and devour every last delicious
rabbit that lives in these cursed woods.'

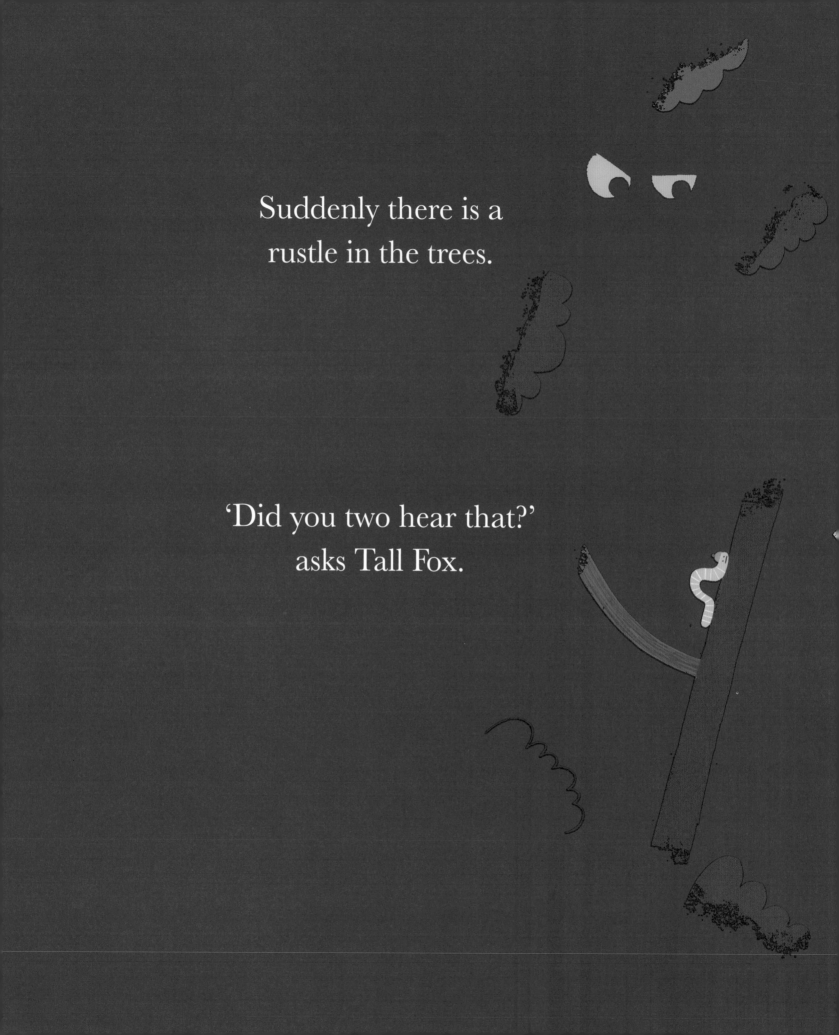

Suddenly there is a
rustle in the trees.

'Did you two hear that?'
asks Tall Fox.

'Maybe it was a rabbit!'
says Round Fox.

'No rabbits here,'
says Tiny Fox.

'The woods are just full of
mysterious mysteries,'
says Tall Fox.

And with the coast most definitely clear,
the three foxes carry on their hunt.

Then they reach the wild river.

'Maybe we should turn back?'
says Tall Fox.

'No!' says Tiny Fox. 'The rabbits
are on the other side. We just need
to get across somehow.'

Tiny Fox spots a steady-looking branch.
'I'll find those rabbits if it's the last thing I do.
Just you wa—'

'Waaaaaagghhhhh!'

Splooooooosh!

'What are you two looking at?!' asks a soggy Tiny Fox.

'Nothing at all!' howls Round Fox.

'YOU NUMBSKULLS ARE THE REASON
WE HAVEN'T CAUGHT ANY RABBITS!'
screams Tiny Fox.

'YOU'RE THE NUMBSKULL!' shouts Round Fox.

'Stop fighting!' says Tall Fox. 'What's that? It looks like...'

RABBITS!!

Here are the woods. The woods are home to three rabbits.

Three rabbits that are on a hunt...

…for foxes.

Stupid, hungry foxes.

For Clare – R.H.

Brimming with creative inspiration, how-to projects, and useful information to enrich your everyday life, Quarto Knows is a favourite destination for those pursuing their interests and passions. Visit our site and dig deeper with our books into your area of interest: Quarto Creates, Quarto Cooks, Quarto Homes, Quarto Lives, Quarto Drives, Quarto Explores, Quarto Gifts, or Quarto Kids.

Inspiring | Educating | Creating | Entertaining

Text and Illustrations © 2019 Rob Hodgson

First published in 2019 by Frances Lincoln Children's Books, an imprint of The Quarto Group. The Old Brewery, 6 Blundell Street, London N7 9BH, United Kingdom. T (0)20 7700 6700 F (0)20 7700 8066 **www.QuartoKnows.com**

A catalogue record for this book is available from the British Library.

ISBN 978-1-78603-274-4

The illustrations were created using mixed and digital media

Set in Baskerville

Published by Rachel Williams
Designed by Andrew Watson
Edited by Katie Cotton
Production by Jenny Cundill and Kate O'Riordan

Manufactured in China

1 3 5 7 9 8 6 4 2

MIX
Paper from responsible sources
FSC® C001701
FSC
www.fsc.org